HIS TO TAKE

an Out of Uniform novella

KATEE ROBERT

Entangled Publishing, LLC
2614 South Timberline Road
Suite 109
Fort Collins, CO 80525
Visit our website at www.entangledpublishing.com.

Brazen is an imprint of Entangled Publishing, LLC. For more information on our titles, visit www.brazenbooks.com.

Edited by Heather Howland
Cover design by Heather Howland
Cover art from iStock

Manufactured in the United States of America

First Edition December 2015

ENTANGLED
BRAZEN

To the Rabble. This one's for you!

Chapter One

Erin Robinson glanced at her phone for the fifth time in five minutes. Unfortunately, the minutes hadn't gone backward and no texts had arrived, which meant only one thing—she'd been stood up. There was no other way to explain her blind date's being over thirty minutes late and not bothering with some sort of reassuring *something* to let her know he wasn't dead in a ditch somewhere. It might be snowing outside, but any citizen in the Wellingford area worth their salt had prepared for the harsh winter months ago. This guy apparently grew up the next town over. If he hadn't put studs on his truck and sandbags in the bed, he was an idiot.

Kind of like I'm an idiot for agreeing to this date in the first place.

She'd only done it to get her mother off her back for a little while. Erin had figured the worst that would happen was that the guy would be an insufferable dick, and she'd spent enough time with guys like that over the years to know how to deal with them.

Being stood up never entered into her realm of

possibilities.

She glanced around Chilly's, hoping she didn't see anyone she knew. That would just be the icing on the humiliation cake she'd been eating for the last month. After she'd turned nineteen and blown out of here with both middle fingers up to move to New York, she'd never once considered that she'd be back here six years later with her tail between her legs, jobless and forced to move back in with her parents. The Wellingford rumor mill hadn't quite figured that out yet, though. *Thank God.* She'd threatened both her parents with a lifetime of therapy bills if they told anyone that she was back for anything other than visiting over the holidays between shows.

Visiting permanently.

Shame stuck in her throat. She should have kept her mouth shut last month when Randy, aka Director Douche, started spouting about her performance as Ariel in *The Little Mermaid.* Everyone knew he was a dick, and she *had* the part. For the first time, she wasn't an understudy or relegated to the background. It was going to be her big break.

But then he'd made Maggie cry. The girl was tough as nails, even if she was only twelve, and he'd stripped all that confidence away with a few sharp words. And that, Erin couldn't deal with silently.

Well, she'd paid for her attitude by getting fired, and then the universe decided to stomp on her while she was down in the form of her landlord kicking her ass to the curb. Apparently he was tired of waiting "just one more month" for her to catch up on rent.

So, here she was, occupying a stool in Chilly's, the one bar worth mentioning in the one-stop town she grew up in. The place where everyone knew everyone else's name—and could recite their family tree back half a dozen generations. The past was never the past here.

"Hey, stranger."

Erin stared at her beer, wondering if the bartender, Gena, had slipped her a little something extra, because there was no other explanation for hearing *that* voice in her ear. *Spend too much time thinking about the past and it'll creep up on you. Next thing I know, I'll be as bad as my parents, constantly living in the glory days.* She took another drink of her beer to buy herself time before she had to turn around and face the fact that either she was hallucinating in a truly magical fashion or, even worse, that Warren Davis was standing right behind her.

Hearing his voice was all it took for her imagination to kick into high gear. She didn't have to look at him to *feel* him at her back, probably wearing that self-satisfied smirk he always seemed to have on his face. Unfortunately, it didn't make him any less attractive. If she concentrated, she could almost catch a whiff of the expensive cologne he favored.

Nothing for it. She had to face the music. She took a fortifying breath and spun on her stool, her heart jumping into her throat in a seriously annoying way. Some things never changed, and apparently her reaction to this particular man was one of them.

It didn't help that he looked… Hell, he looked *really* good. His hair was shorn close to his head in the traditional Marine style, but it was all too easy to picture the way it curled when he let too long go between haircuts. Every time she went back to New York after visiting home, she'd half convinced herself that his dark brown eyes couldn't possibly be as soulful as she remembered—and every time she was wrong. And his mouth…

Erin flushed and reached for her beer again. She had firsthand knowledge of just how devastating that mouth could be—both in and out of the bedroom.

Stop it. Stop it right now.

The last thing she had the energy to do was dredge up the attitude necessary to deal with Warren, but she tried anyway. "Hey, yourself."

"Nice comeback." He dropped onto the stool next to her.

That was another thing she almost always managed to forget—how damn aggravating the man could be. Five seconds in his presence and she was transported back to when she was a hotheaded nineteen-year-old with more hormones than sense, and the one wild summer they'd spent together. Erin glared. "Find another seat. This one is taken."

"By your imaginary friend?" He nodded at Gena. "You've been sitting alone for half an hour with no one in sight. If he's not here by now, he's not coming."

He'd been here the entire time, watching her? *How did I miss him?* Her face went hot enough to scald. It was bad enough knowing she'd been stood up—it was a thousand times worse to know that *he* had witnessed it. "You're unbelievable. I'm waiting for Marcy."

"Liar. She and Aaron are out of town until tomorrow." He rubbed a hand over his mouth, his dark eyes shining with amusement. "Which is a damn good thing, because your brother still hasn't gotten over his love of giving me speeding tickets after my granddad set Marcy and I up a while back."

Erin looked away, fighting the urge to smile. Marcy had told her about that, and she'd be lying if she said it didn't make her day a little bit brighter to know that her brother went out of his way to shit on Warren's day when he could. "You should consider yourself lucky. If he knew half of the stuff you pulled with me when we first met, he'd kill you." But her brother didn't know. No one knew—not even her best friend, Marcy. The forbidden and secret aspect of their relationship—if it could be called that—had been part of the attraction back then.

Now it just felt stupid.

"No, he wouldn't." He accepted the beer Gena set in front of him with a smile. "He might whup your ass for getting involved with me, but Aaron is too honorable to stoop to something like murder for his rebellious Mini Me."

Mini Me. One of the many hated nicknames that she'd never been able to escape because of her parents' questionable taste in naming their son and daughter versions of the same damn name. There was no excuse for that kind of lunacy. The best she could tell, her mother had insisted they name their second child Erin out of sheer stubbornness. Pregnancy-related hormones did weird things to the brain—she'd seen that well enough when Marcy was knocked up—and her mother had never met a mistake she was willing to admit to. So despite her father's pleading, she'd refused to change the initial name on the birth certificate.

Which is how Aaron and Erin came to be.

The town took it in stride like it did most of the locals' quirks, and everyone and their dog had taken to fondly calling Erin some variation of "Mini Me." As if she weren't her own entity. She'd half thought that it would change after Aaron graduated and went off to join the Army.

She should have known better.

Just like she should have known that engaging Warren in any type of conversation was a mistake. It ended only one of two ways, neither of which she had the wherewithal to deal with.

Erin finished off her beer. "As fun as this has been, I'm leaving." She carefully counted out her last few five-dollar bills and set them on the counter next to her beer. *I am so broke, it's not even funny. Thought I might at least get a free meal out of this damn date, and here I am, paying for my own drinks.* It was time to get out of here. The longer she stayed in Warren's presence, the closer she came to losing what little self-control she had. Right now she was leaning toward snarking that smug expression right off his Marine face, but she knew herself well enough to know that could flip like a switch. And the *last* thing she needed was to make the mistake of falling back into bed with Warren Davis. With her current luck, it would be the straw that broke the proverbial camel's back.

It didn't matter how many times she'd told herself the same thing over the years and then promptly ignored her own advice. She always woke up the next morning in a pit of self-loathing and angst — which was why she'd taken to avoiding him over the last year. When the hurt started outweighing the pleasure, it was time to kick the habit.

She pushed to her feet, trying to ignore the way he did the same. "I mean it, Warren."

"When did you become a coward?"

"I'm not a goddamn coward." She froze. *How does he always manage to do that?* A few words and he was under her skin, poking at things she thought she was too mature to be riled by. She turned around to face him and — surprise, surprise — he was wearing that little smirk that made her breathing pick up. *Not this time, Erin. You know better, remember?* "Knowing a losing battle when I see it isn't cowardly. It's smart."

Warren searched her face, and for a second, she thought he'd drop the smart-ass act, but then the corner of his mouth quirked up. "So who was the poor shmuck you scared away? Anyone I know?"

Irritation got the best of her — again — and she spoke without thinking, "And why is it always my fault? I didn't do a damn thing to the guy." She hadn't done more than respond to his texts. Yeah, she might have been a little short with him, and maybe she corrected his atrocious grammar once or twice, but how was she supposed to take this guy seriously when he used emoticons and shortened all his words to their letter counterparts? It was like texting with a teenager.

"Maybe he was intimidated."

She glared. "You know damn well that's not the case." She *wished* she could be intimidating. Her life would have gone a whole lot differently if that was something she could pull off, but with her shoulder-length curly brown hair, freckles, and wide hazel eyes, she'd grown up with comments about how delicate and breakable she looked. It just made her more fiercely determined to prove everyone wrong.

"I don't know, Freckles." He grinned suddenly. "You've got me shaking in my boots."

Hearing his pet name for her on his lips was a jolt she needed like another hole in the head. Erin looked him up and down, keeping her expression unimpressed despite the way the man filled out a thermal shirt. And those jeans... *Get a hold of yourself.* "You're not wearing boots." She turned back for the door.

"What are you doing back in town?"

Nope. No way was she doing this. She motioned to the Christmas lights strung up over every available beam in the room. "That's a stupid question. It's Christmas in two days."

Now that she mentioned it, that explained what Warren was doing back in town. He liked to come home during the holidays to visit his grandfather, Old Joe. It was part of the reason she'd made excuses last year to come in for the minimum time necessary to meet her familial obligations—this was the one time of year she was guaranteed to see the man if she wasn't careful.

"See you around." *But hopefully not too much.* Erin kept her head high as she pushed through the door and out into the frozen night. Though it was exactly what she wanted, she couldn't help feeling a smidgen of disappointment when she realized he wasn't following her.

Chapter Two

Warren watched Erin go and then turned back to his beer. He shouldn't have poked at her, but hell if he could resist approaching her when she was sitting all alone with that lost look on her face. The woman he knew didn't hold still long enough to be lost, so it was disconcerting in a big way to realize that something so fundamental about her might have changed when he wasn't paying attention.

So he'd done the one thing he knew would snap her out of it.

Even then, it hadn't fully chased that expression off her face. She was like a boxer who'd taken a ringer and was against the ropes. He didn't like it. He didn't like it one bit. Warren took another pull from his beer. It wasn't his goddamn business. Nothing about Erin Robinson was—something she'd made damn sure he knew time and time again over the years. He might have access to her body, but she never let him past the surface after that first summer. They'd get together for wild sex in whatever place was available—closets, bathrooms, one particularly memorable time on a tractor—and the next morning she'd slip out of bed and walk away.

And hell if she didn't take a little piece of him every time she did.

Gena stopped in front of him and leaned against the bar. "How long are you back in town this time?"

There was no missing the interest in her eyes, but he couldn't find an answering spark inside him. Even a year ago, he might have considered taking a stab at it. But that was before his last tour in Afghanistan, before... He didn't touch his newest scar—a bullet wound just above his hip—but it was a near thing. That injury had changed his course, whether he wanted it to or not.

It had put a lot of shit into perspective while he was lying in the hospital, wondering if he was going to die.

One of those things was Erin.

She was fire and lightning, all bottled up in a package that was deceptively innocent-looking. A man who didn't know better would be caught flat-footed when she went from sweet to pit bull in the space of a heartbeat. The contradiction was part of what had attracted Warren to her in the first place. It was one of the things that kept him coming back for more, no matter that she seemed determined to keep him at a distance.

He glanced up and realized he'd been so lost in thought, he hadn't responded to Gena. "Just for the holidays." Old Joe was town patriarch in a lot of ways, but the holidays had a way of bringing out the loneliness when people weren't paying attention. With Warren's parents off in... He thought hard. Where were they this month? India? Thailand? Brazil? He'd lost track. In a week or two, a postcard would show up with another exotic location on it and a short note from them. These days they even managed to pick up the phone every few months.

His parents suffered from a wanderlust that was rivaled only by their love for each other. Growing up, they'd hauled him along like a well-loved teddy bear—and paid him about as much attention. He'd spent his formative years in Mexico, Russia, Chile, and half a dozen other places scattered around the world. The only constant had been when they sent him back here for a few weeks a year to spend time with Old Joe. Even with so little time, his granddad had become his rock in a lot of ways.

In a life where everything around him was a never-ceasing wind, that consistency was priceless.

So he came home every holiday season to spend time with the old man. His granddad always had a whole new batch of stories to tell. It had been one of Warren's favorite times of year growing up, and it was even more so in a lot of ways now.

Especially now that he was looking for a life that was more rocklike than windblown.

Disappointment flickered over Gena's face, but she masked it quickly. "Mark my words, Warren Davis—someday you're going to settle down in Wellingford for good."

"Maybe someday." Sooner than anyone realized. He'd told his granddad about his plans, but it wasn't public knowledge. Not yet, at least. He finished off his beer and dropped a twenty on the bar. Though he knew better, he asked, "You see Erin Robinson around here much?"

"Just the last month." She shrugged. "She's between shows or something."

That made sense, though he'd never known her to come back here for longer than strictly necessary since that first summer they spent together. Ever since he could remember, she'd had her eyes to the stars and her plans for moving to New York and becoming a famous Broadway star. She hadn't done too bad for herself, but all his knowledge was second- and thirdhand, so there was no telling.

He glanced at the door and frowned. There had been something off about her tonight. He'd thought it was just being stood up—though fuck if *that* didn't aggravate the hell out of him. What kind of idiot stood up Erin Robinson? She was dynamite. A guy got a chance with a woman like that, and he jumped at it with both hands.

So why haven't I?

That was the damn question, wasn't it? He'd already decided that he cared about Erin. There was no time like the present to start putting shit into motion to see if it was even worth pursuing.

He headed out into the night and pulled out his phone, dialing before he could talk himself out of it. One little phone call wouldn't hurt either of them any. *Liar.* He barely gave Erin time to say hello before he spoke. "I have an idea."

"Not interested."

"Yes, you are. Unless you've lost your edge in your old age." He put just enough arrogant tone into the last to make her see red. It had never failed him before—if there was one thing Erin had in spades, it was pride.

Sure enough, she hissed out a breath. "No more than you joining the Marines has made you an idiot jarhead—oh wait, you were like that before you joined."

There was that fire he was used to. "Damn, Freckles, I think that was almost a compliment." He grinned. "Meet me down at the coffee shop."

"It's closed."

He had her, hook, line, and sinker. "See you in ten." Warren hung up and grinned. He might be ready to go all-in with the woman, but she'd have to be eased into the idea. If he played his cards right, by the end of the night, she'd see exactly how great they could be together—and this time maybe she wouldn't be so eager to walk away.

He slipped his phone into his pocket and meandered down Main Street. Even in the cold front that had blown in today, the town wasn't completely deserted. There was Miss

Nora, walking her beast of a dog. She waved as she passed, but for once didn't stop to talk. Warren flicked up his collar to keep the wind off the back of his neck and crossed the street to where the warm lights of the coffee shop bathed the sidewalk. Even closed up, it was a beacon in the middle of the shadows cast by the few streetlights.

Should have told her to meet me in the Diner.

Except he didn't want an audience for this, and there was sure to be one there. The last thing he wanted was his granddad's knowing looks and sly comments about what a good girl Erin was. They'd never officially dated and no one else in town knew that they'd dicked around at all, but Old Joe didn't miss much. No one had been more heartbroken than Warren's granddad when they didn't immediately get married and pop out a few kids. Old Joe made more comments than he could count about how he always thought Warren and Erin would make a great couple.

We were too young back then. Now we aren't.

He turned at the sound of footsteps in time to see her come round the corner, her shoulders hunched against the cold, her curly hair shoved up under a neon-green knit hat that, if he didn't miss his guess, her mom had made for her. He'd recognize those missed stitches anywhere. What the woman lacked in skill, she made up for in bright colors and sheer enthusiasm.

Erin scowled when she caught sight of him. "This had better be good. I was almost home."

It was less than half a mile walk from Main Street to her parents' house on the outskirts of town. He raised his eyebrows. "You really are getting old if you're headed home before midnight."

She made a show of looking around. "Right. Because Wellingford is such a hot spot of activity at this hour." She sighed. "You know what? This was a mistake."

"Wait." He heard desperation in his voice and tempered it down. "You haven't even heard what I'm proposing."

"I don't have to. I know you. And as great as an hour of hot sweaty sex would be, I'm not in the mood."

That, more than anything else, confirmed there was something wrong. He tamped down the urge to ask what it was. They weren't that kind of friends. Not yet. They were two people who'd hooked up a handful of times in the last six years. That was it.

That was what he was trying to change.

So he nudged her shoulder, hating that the winter made so many layers necessary. It was only his imagination making him think he could feel the heat of her body through her coat from that tiny touch. "Truth or dare, Freckles?"

Her jaw dropped. "You're joking."

"We haven't done it in years." Not since the night they met.

"Right. Because we're grown-ass adults, and truth or dare is for kids."

He watched the memories reflected in her hazel eyes. Truth or dare was how they'd gotten started in the first place. They'd been with a group of friends down at Mill Creek and someone had suggested the game. It had been a wild night of the kind of trouble only teenagers could get into, and it had culminated out in the middle of the creek where another of their friends dared Erin to kiss Warren.

And, holy fuck, had she kissed him.

His body heated, his cock going rock hard at the memory of her soft lips against his. There had been no hesitation even back then. Once Erin decided on a course, she went after it a thousand percent.

After that kiss, she'd decided she wanted Warren.

He'd been completely on board with that idea. The following months had been the most insane of his life. They couldn't get enough of each other, and he couldn't begin to count the times they'd almost been caught. Warren would like to chalk it up to teenage hormones, but here he was, staring at Erin's mouth and wondering if the last year had changed things or if he'd kiss her and get a taste of the wintergreen gum she always seemed to be chewing.

"Stop looking at me like that."

"No." He realized what he'd said and shook his head. *Reel it back in, Davis.* "Truth or dare?"

For a long moment, he thought she'd tell him to take a hike. Hell, he'd deserve it if she did. She didn't owe him a goddamn thing, let alone to play a game straight from the past they both went out of their way not to think too hard about.

But then Erin licked her lips. "Dare."

Got you, Freckles.

Chapter Three

This was such a mistake it wasn't even funny. Erin crossed her arms over her chest, waiting for Warren to tell her what her dare would be. This game had started them down the path all those years ago, so to start playing tonight, when she was feeling raw and vulnerable, was probably the worst idea she'd had in a long time.

But she'd already picked up the gauntlet he'd thrown down. Changing her mind now meant she'd lose, and all she seemed to have left these days was her pride. She couldn't back down. Not now. Not until she'd won.

Maybe if I can do this tonight, I can finally start to get control of my life again. It could be a step in the right direction.

And maybe she was just looking for an excuse to get into some trouble with Warren Davis.

He grinned, that quick and easy expression that always meant trouble in the best way possible. She tried to ignore that one look from him could make her stomach erupt into a cloud of butterflies. Warren jerked a thumb over his shoulder. "Flash the sheriff."

Erin blinked. "Uh, what?"

"You heard me, Freckles." He moved to the side and she saw the sheriff's cruiser crawling down the street. It was still several blocks away, but if she was going to do the dare, she had to move quickly.

"You are such an asshole." She shrugged out of her coat and shoved it at him, part of her wondering why the hell she was doing this. All she had to do was walk away. She was twenty-five goddamn years old—too old to be indulging in a pissing contest with a guy who was supposed to be ancient history. Erin stepped to the curb.

"And if you get arrested, you automatically lose."

She shot a look over her shoulder. "Give me some credit. Sheriff Flannery might not be a geezer like Sheriff Jones was, but I'm not going to stand around waiting to get arrested." She turned back in time to see the patrol car hit their block. It was now or never.

Bracing herself against the cold, she grabbed the bottom of her shirt and jerked it and her bra up to her neck as the headlights hit her body. Her breasts instantly broke out in goose bumps and her nipples pebbled as the cold seared straight to her bones. She held her breath for half a second, and then jerked her clothes back into place.

Right about the same time that the patrol car let loose a chirp that evolved into sirens, the blue and red lights on the roof flashing.

Warren grabbed her arm. "Run!"

"You run." She snatched her coat out of his arms and took off, ducking down the alley between the coffee shop and the post office, her boots hitting the ground in a rhythm that matched Warren's half a second behind her.

Erin slid around the corner and kept going, crossing Second Street and heading for the residential area behind it. She cut across two front lawns and dived behind the huge lilac bushes Miss Nora kept in her front yard, breathing hard. The mass of thin branches and the snow covering them should be more than enough to hide them. She hoped. Then Warren was there, crowding against her, too close and somehow not close enough. She shivered, refusing to look at him because she feared what he'd see on her face.

Adrenaline. That's all this is.

Right. She'd just run from a cop. Erin huffed out a laugh as the patrol car cruised past them, the sirens now silent. *That was close.* Sheriff Flannery was a pretty decent guy, so she doubted he'd try too hard to find her—especially since no one else was subject to her public nudity—but her heart still raced from the short chase.

Beside her, Warren chuckled. "Just like old times, huh?"

Just like old times and yet completely different. They weren't kids anymore. He was a Marine now, and she was a failed Broadway actress. The reminder left her colder than the snow beneath her.

Desperate to reclaim the free feeling that had just left her, she said, "Truth or dare?"

"You know me well enough to know that." His smile was a flash of white teeth in the shadows. "Dare."

"Kiss me." The words were out before she could think better of them, before she could take them back to protect herself. *This was why you stopped the fling with him. He makes you forget yourself.* Knowing that was all well and good in the warm light of day. Right now, huddled behind a bush in Miss Nora's front yard, she didn't care about any of it.

All she cared about tonight was forgetting. Reality would still be there tomorrow, no matter how much she wanted to escape it. Warren offered a chance to slip into a fantasy of "what if?" for a little while. It wouldn't ultimately change anything between them. It never did. But that didn't matter in this moment.

Warren's cold hand at the back of her neck startled her out of her mental spiral. His breath warmed her lips a second before his mouth took hers. Considering their current location, the kiss should have been uncomfortable and awkward, but apparently he hadn't gotten the memo.

He nipped her bottom lip, using her moan to gain access to her mouth. They hadn't so much as touched in over a year, but that didn't seem to matter with his tongue stroking along hers in that heady way. The intervening time disappeared just like it always had in the past, and suddenly she was nineteen again, her body responding and her hormones sweeping away what little common sense she could call her own.

Erin grabbed the front of his coat, needing to be closer, to feel skin against skin, to follow through on the promise of his mouth on hers. She barely registered Warren moving back until he created some actual distance between them. "Damn, Freckles, that was fun."

Fun… It took her brain far too long to catch up. *Just a kiss, you idiot.* "Uh…" She shook her head, trying to focus. "I don't… Give me a second."

"You have a second." He rose and offered her his hand. "Let's get out of here before Miss Nora gets back."

The fact that the kiss obviously hadn't affected him the same way it had her doused the last of the fuzziness in her head. She ignored his outstretched hand and shoved to her feet. As much as part of her wanted to just walk away, she'd already committed to seeing this through.

And he was right—being here when Miss Nora got back was a mistake. The woman was right at the center of the Wellingford gossip mill, and what she knew, the rest of the town would inside of twelve hours.

The very *last* thing Erin needed was for her parents—or, worse, her brother—to start asking uncomfortable questions about why she was running around at all hours of the night with one Warren Davis. *Mom would be so thrilled at the chance of seeing me married off to become someone else's problem.*

That wasn't fair. Her parents loved her dearly. It wasn't their fault she'd always been a fish out of water when it came to the rest of her family. Aside from her mom's temporary, pregnancy-induced insanity when it came to naming Erin, they'd been a solid pillar for her entire life. And Aaron was as steady as time itself. The craziest thing he'd ever done was go off and join the Army, and he'd come right back to Wellingford after his time was served.

Then there was Erin. The wild child. The one with drama in her blood. The one who didn't fit in.

It had been true when she was a kid, and it was just as true now. Her parents tried. Good lord, they tried. But they just didn't get her any more than she got them. To them, it was simple—things had gone south in New York, which was a sign that it was time for her to come home and settle down.

Settle down.

It sounded like a death sentence from where Erin was sitting.

What am I going to do? The only thing I ever wanted was to be a Broadway actress. Do I go back to New York and start over? Or do I… What? Stay here, get married, get knocked up, and join the PTA?

There had to be some middle ground between the two. She just had to find it.

She was so wrapped up in the misery going on inside her head, she didn't pay attention where they were going until she took a step and sank into snow up to her knees. Erin looked around, frowning. They'd hit the edge of town. There was nothing out here but trees and the occasional farm.

Which apparently was where they were headed.

Warren dragged her across the small field and into the barn situated away from the road. It was slow going through the knee-deep snow, even with him breaking a path for her to follow. She jerked her hand out of his—*when had he taken her hand?*—and looked around. "The Joneses' old barn? Really?" she turned back to ask, and inhaled sharply when she found him a mere breath away. This close, she could smell the winter on his skin, which should have been expected since they'd just been traipsing around in the snow, but somehow managed to make her toes curl in her boots all the same. "I—"

He nudged her over to a workbench against the far wall—a grand total of five steps away. It wasn't as cold as it was outside, but her breath still ghosted the air in front of her. "I really don't think Sheriff Flannery is still looking for us."

"Probably not." He guided her to sit on the bench.

Erin looked around. "Since we're on the same page, why are we hiding in the Joneses' old barn? I know Wellingford is pretty countrified but this is ridiculous." They'd built a bigger, newer barn on the other side of their property last year, so this one was only being used for extra storage and was guaranteed to be deserted, but that didn't mean she wanted to camp out in it. She wanted to keep moving, to get back into town and back to their game. The faster he dealt out another dare to her, the faster she could win and move on with her life.

He went to his knees in front of her, his big body sliding between her thighs and spreading her legs. "I still have my dare to complete."

"Uh, no, you don't. You completed it back in Miss Nora's front yard." She pointed even as hurt blossomed in her chest. That kiss had been freaking amazing and he was acting like it hadn't happened at all.

He shot her a look that stole her breath, his dark eyes so heated it was a wonder she didn't melt into a puddle at his feet. "That wasn't a kiss."

"I was there. Pretty sure it was a kiss."

He pulled off one of her boots and then the other, and she

was so shocked that she let him. Warren ran his hands up her legs, making her wish she'd worn something flimsier than her favorite pair of jeans. "I don't know who you've been kissing over the last year, but they obviously haven't been doing it properly."

She bit her lip when his chilled fingers brushed the top of her jeans, slipping beneath her shirt to stroke along her skin. Why was she trying to argue her way out of this…whatever it was? "I've been kissed plenty fine in the last year."

"No, you haven't." He abruptly tightened his grip and jerked her to the very edge of the bench.

Her breath stalled out, and she could only watch as he unbuttoned her jeans and worked them down her legs, never taking his gaze from her face. Erin licked her lips. "How would you know?"

"Because, Freckles, you haven't been kissed by me."

Chapter Four

Warren would have backed off any other time, but tonight was his Hail Mary pass at Erin, and he was pulling out all the stops. Sex had always been uncomplicated with them—the only thing she'd accept from him freely, with no questions asked.

And, fuck, he thought he might die if he didn't get his hands on her bare skin again.

He finished sliding her jeans off her legs and dropped them on the ground behind him. She had this look on her face, like she was nervous, which had him asking, "Do you want me to stop?"

"Seriously?"

He forced himself to stop touching her and sit back on his heels. "Seriously."

"You're unbelievable." Erin shook her head. "You can't throw out a line like that and then ask me if I want you to stop." When he didn't immediately move closer, she rolled her eyes. "No, genius. I don't want you to stop."

That was all he needed to know. He closed the distance

between them and dealt her a punishing kiss in response. Kissing Erin had always been the easiest thing in the world, and the feel of her, all hot and warm, in his arms was enough to drive a better man than him to distraction. He tangled his fingers in her hair and tilted her head back. "About that kiss…"

"For the millionth time, we already kissed."

He liked how breathy her voice was and how unfocused her hazel eyes became. He liked it a lot. "Wrong." He licked and nibbled his way down her throat, unzipping her coat and pushing it down her arms. Her shirt was next, over her head and joining her jeans on the floor. Then there was only her bra and panties. He eyed the blue cotton with little pink flowers on it. "Nice."

"Shut up."

He kissed down her stomach. Her panties weren't an exact match for her bra, but their pink color was the same as the flowers. The whole effect was unexpectedly devastating. He ran his thumbs just outside the line of fabric. "Prepare yourself, Freckles." He didn't give her a chance to respond before he ducked his head and pressed an openmouthed kiss to the fabric covering her. Her responding moan was music to his ears, but he was too lost in being this close to her after a long year of exile.

If he didn't play his cards right tonight, he might never get a chance like this again.

Warren hooked a thumb inside her panties and dragged them to the side, baring her to him. His first taste made him growl. "You're wet for me."

"Stop talking and kiss me." Her hands snaked over his head to tow him closer, as if he needed any further motivation.

He sucked on her clit, working her just like he knew she wanted, her cries only driving him on. It wouldn't take much more of this to make her come, and he wanted the taste of her pleasure on his tongue more than he wanted his next breath. "These panties have to go." He tore himself away from her long enough to yank them down her legs, and then he was back, fucking her with his tongue as her hips rose off the table to meet him halfway.

"Warren." His name was a gasp on her lips. "Warren, wait."

He froze, fingers digging into her thighs, mouth against her center. She didn't give him a chance to ask her again if she wanted him to stop. Erin tugged on his shirt. "I want you inside me when I come."

The world hazed out in a cascade of lust that made it hard to focus. He rested his forehead on her stomach, forcing himself to stop and *think*. There was nothing he wanted more than to shuck off his pants and fuck her until she was screaming and coming around his cock. Even thinking about it was enough to have his balls tightening in anticipation.

Not yet.

He had to keep this centered on their game, centered on making her want more. If they had sex now, there was nothing keeping her from walking away from him tonight like she had every other time they'd hooked up.

So he grabbed her hands and used one of his to pin her wrists to the small of her back. "A kiss, Freckles. That's all you get." *For now.* Before she could protest again, he went back to her pussy, licking and sucking and driving her ruthlessly toward orgasm.

But he didn't let her reach that final completion.

Her cries grew louder, and Warren eased back, slowing his pace. He used his free hand to spread her folds, spending precious minutes exploring her there.

"Goddamn it, you fucking tease." She pulled against his hold, but he wasn't about to let her take the reins. He was in the driver's seat tonight, whether she liked it or not.

"You sound so fucking sexy when you're frustrated." He flicked her clit with his tongue, knowing damn well that it wasn't enough to do more than infuriate her.

"Bastard!" It was more of a moan than a yell.

He lifted his head. "I can stop…"

"Don't you dare." She bit her lip, looking down her body at him. "Stop teasing me. Please."

He almost ignored the plea. Almost. But the sight of her pale skin broken out in goose bumps brought him back to himself. *We're in a goddamn barn. Much more of this and the shivers racking her body aren't going to be because she's turned on.*

As much as he wanted to keep this up, it would have to wait. Warren tightened his grip on her and moved back to her clit, flicking and circling and sucking as she went wild against him. He didn't stop, didn't slow down, didn't do a damn thing that would give her room to breathe. Instead, he drove her unrelentingly toward orgasm, a primal part of him howling in satisfaction at the wild way she cried his name when she came.

She's mine. She just doesn't know it yet.

Chapter Five

Erin couldn't believe she'd just come screaming Warren's name when less than an hour ago, she was promising herself she would avoid doing exactly that. So much for her plan to use him as her first step to get her life back on track. Instead, this was yet another mistake in a long line of questionable decisions she'd made that had brought her to exactly this place at exactly this time. It was as if someone had thrown a bucket of cold water on her.

She pushed him away and went for her pants, her legs still shaking from the force of her orgasm. Looking at him there on his knees, his dark eyes lit with desire as he took in every inch of her, made her want to throw caution to the wind and tackle him to the ground.

No. You already debased yourself by begging him to fuck you, and he said no. *This is about the goddamn game, and you'd be a fool to forget that.* She cursed mentally. *I'm batting a thousand at life right now.* "That was nice."

"Nice." He climbed to his feet and watched her, the cold not seeming to bother him in the least. "You just came screaming my name and 'nice' is the best you can do?"

"I just call it like I see it." And she was a goddamn liar. There'd been nothing *nice* about what he just did to her. It was hot and dirty and all sorts of wrong and right twisted up into deliciousness. But she couldn't tell him that without opening the door for another round, which was *not* in the cards tonight. She pulled her jeans on. "And how I see it was that was nice."

"You're something else."

"Been hearing that all my life." And usually in exactly that tone of voice. It wasn't fair to lay a lifetime of baggage at Warren's feet, but he always seemed to dredge up her issues whenever they said more than two words to each other. The sex…the sex was so much simpler. If they could have just kept it physical, maybe being around him wouldn't feel so damn confusing.

Maybe.

She yanked on her boots and stood. The look on his face said it all. He wasn't done with her. Her heart skipped a beat, even as her head kicked into panic to avoid whatever he was opening his mouth to say. She blurted out the first thing that came to mind. "Your turn."

"What?"

This was her chance. *Just walk away. The night has already gone off the rails if you're crazy enough to flash the damn sheriff and then nearly get busy in a freaking* barn. *You aren't nineteen anymore, no matter how much it feels like it right now.*

It was too late to go back, though. It had been too late the second she went back to New York after that summer of pure bliss she spent with him, a guy who'd already seen more of the world as a teenager than she could even begin to imagine. They were never meant to be together, but it was hard to remember that when his mouth and hands were on her. It was impossible to come back to Wellingford and not fish for information about him—Where was he stationed? Was he still doing okay? Was he going to be sent on yet another tour of Iraq or Afghanistan?—and that curiosity and worry hadn't just magically stopped when they took the sex out of the equation. If they started up again, it would be so much worse.

Which meant she had to get through the night without a repeat of what they'd just done. "Or, really, it's my turn. I pick dare, by the way."

His mouth tightened. "That's how it's going to be, then."

She started to mouth off, but sighed and shrugged into her coat. "That's how it always is, Warren." She'd spent a significant time working *not* to think about what her life would be like if they were different people in different circumstances. If he were willing to settle in one place that wasn't Wellingford. If she were willing to put aside the dreams that led her to New York. If he didn't love this town so much. If this town didn't make her feel like she was wearing a sweater that was two sizes too small.

But she couldn't spend her life hanging her hopes on what-ifs.

Especially when that was how she'd gotten into her current mess to begin with.

"Fine. You want a dare, you got it." He snatched her hat off the ground and shoved it into her hands. "Come on."

All I have to do to end this is call the whole thing off. But doing that meant losing, and she needed to win this now more than ever. That was why she followed Warren back out into the snowy night. It certainly wasn't because she wasn't willing to put an end to their night together. Nope. Not even a little bit.

Chapter Six

Anger followed Warren, dogging his steps as he stalked across the field and back toward town. He didn't look behind him to see if Erin was following. She was. God forbid she sit down and enjoy the afterglow. No, Erin had to panic and throw up whatever barriers between them she could come up with. Tonight, that was the game.

You knew this wasn't going to be easy.

Yeah, he had. But that didn't make it any easier to stomach. He felt edgy and like he was in danger of snapping. Warren took a deep breath and did his damnedest to rein it in. It took the better part of ten minutes to reach Main Street again, and the walk didn't do a single thing to cool his temper. He looked around. The sheriff wasn't in sight. *That's something, at least.*

He started to turn back to her, but stopped when his gaze landed on the water tower tucked back behind the buildings lining the street. He didn't need light to know the faded white tower was covered in decades' worth of graffiti, each graduating class determined to leave their mark, whether they were leaving Wellingford in the rearview or settling here for good.

He pointed. "Climb that."

"*What?*"

The shock in her voice slammed him back into reality. What the fuck was he thinking? Erin was terrified of heights. While twenty feet up wasn't a big deal to him, it would be to her. During that one summer together, she'd let herself be egged into cliff jumping by one of the asshole local boys, and she'd had a panic attack once she reached the top. He'd barely been able to get her back down again without having to call someone for help.

Warren rubbed a hand over his face, feeling like the world's biggest asshole. *So much for pulling out all the stops of seduction. She pricks your pride and the first thing you do is throw her under the bus. Way to be an asshole.* "Never mind."

"Oh, no you don't." She stopped next to him, her gaze trained on the water tower. "You want to be a dick and make me climb the water tower, fine. I'll do it."

"Erin—" What the hell were they doing? He'd wanted to reclaim some of that first crazy summer together, and it seemed like with each dare, they spiraled a bit further out of control. *Can't just ask a woman on a date, can you, Davis? You have to challenge her to a game that's going to get one or both of you arrested and has you acting like a goddamn fool.*

"The rules are what they are. No changing dares once you put them out there." She marched across the street and moved around the antiques store, forcing him to hurry to keep up.

"Fuck the rules."

She stopped so suddenly, he almost ran into her, and she spun to face him. "I don't need your pity and I don't need you to go easy on me." Then she was gone, striding to the ladder of the water tower and hauling herself off the ground.

Warren didn't hesitate. He went after her. "You're being stupid."

Her voice drifted down from above him as she hauled herself higher. "I'm not the stupid one in this equation."

He wished he could argue that, but she had a point. He'd pushed her into this game for his own reasons, and *he'd* been the one to bring them to the edge again and again. He knew she wanted her space from him—the fact that she'd gone out of her way to avoid him the last time they saw each other spoke volumes—and he'd still dragged her into the barn. Then, when her reaction hurt his pride, he acted like a little bitch by daring her to do something he knew would scare the shit out of her.

This was so not how his plans for the night were supposed to go.

I am such an asshole.

Above him, she reached the section that lined the circumference of the tower and moved out of the way so he could follow. Erin sat down with her back against the cold metal tower, her breath coming too fast for it to be exertion from the climb. "This was such a dumb idea."

"I'm not arguing that." He sat next to her. "This dare was a dick move. I'm sorry."

"I can handle it."

He didn't have any doubts of that. Ever since he'd met her, Erin was always the first to charge into a situation, and she never let impossible odds dissuade her from what she wanted. He was pretty sure she'd made a name for herself on Broadway over the last few years through sheer stubbornness. "That's not the point."

"Then what *is* the point?" She still didn't look at him, her gaze trained on something on the horizon.

Hell, he didn't know. This whole plan was starting to look dumber and dumber as the night went on. She might be a bit of an adrenaline junkie, but he doubted making her climb this tower was the way to her heart. "Why are you really back in town, Freckles? It's not because of the holidays, is it?"

She went ramrod straight next to him. "I don't know what you're talking about."

If he'd had any doubts before, he didn't now. The questions were just a shot in the dark, but apparently he'd struck gold. "What happened?"

"I don't remember picking truth." She laughed, the sound harsh and forced. "It's not your turn anymore, Warren. It's mine. Truth or dare?"

He gritted his teeth. He didn't want to fall back to the game. He wanted to have a real fucking conversation for once in their lives. But as usual, Erin wasn't playing ball. *What did you expect?*

So he decided to throw her a curve ball. "Truth."

She whipped around to glare at him. "You're joking."

"Serious as a heart attack." Maybe he'd been going about this the wrong way. If he wanted Erin to open up to him, he'd have to do it first.

He wanted her. He hadn't had anything as meaningful with another woman—he hadn't had anything come close. Erin simply flat-out did it for him, and no one else could compare. He just had to get *her* to admit that. She shivered, and he instantly felt even more like a dickhead. "How about we get off this thing and somewhere warmer before you start with the third degree?"

"You're the one who picked truth." But she was already moving to the ladder. He didn't offer to help as she scrambled down to the ground, and he pretended not to notice how pale she was beneath her bright green hat. Erin wouldn't thank him for pointing out her fear again, and she might be pissed enough to call quits to the whole night.

She brushed the snow off her gloves. "Where to?"

"The Diner. Coffee's on me."

She raised her eyebrows. "Is that some sort of innuendo

that's supposed to make me think I'll be up late?"

"Freckles, you've spent nearly a decade living in New York. You people exist on coffee alone."

A shadow passed over her face, but it was gone before he had the chance to figure out if he'd imagined it or not. "Caught me. Can't be the city that never sleeps without basically having an IV of caffeine." She started for Main Street. "Let's get this show on the road."

Warren followed, wondering what exactly he'd missed. She loved New York. Maybe she was back here for longer than she'd like to be—which, for Erin, was anything more than twenty-four hours—but it wasn't like she'd moved back permanently.

Was it?

Chapter Seven

The warmth of The Diner nearly made Erin whimper. She pulled off her gloves and slid into an empty booth. Things were happening too quickly. First Warren had stripped her bare—in more ways than one—with the outstanding oral. And now he was asking questions that hit entirely too close to home. The only reason she'd agreed to this stupid idea in the first place was so that she could forget how shitty her life had become for a night.

And, yeah, maybe she'd wanted to spend some time with the infuriating man. She was chalking *that* one up to temporary insanity. There was no other excuse for it.

She took off her hat and dropped it on top of her gloves. Her coat could wait until the heat had worked its way into her bones. She wished she could blame her shakes on the chill, but it wasn't even close to the truth.

Thank God Warren decided to be such an ass, or I never would have made it up and down that ladder.

That, and she hadn't looked down once. Her fear of heights wasn't as crippling as it had been when she was a teenager, but being more than ten feet off the ground still made her woozy if she wasn't careful. She'd barely sat back when the waitress, Dorothy, appeared, a speculative gleam in her eye. "Fancy seeing you two in here."

Good God. She forced a smile even though the last thing she felt was happy. They should have picked somewhere—anywhere—else to warm up. The damn Joneses' barn would have been a better alternative than stepping into the one place guaranteed to get the gossip mill churning.

Sure enough, Dorothy pinned her with a look. "So, Mini Me, how long are you back in town this time? Seems like it's been longer than a weekend."

It was only a matter of time before her failure and humiliation were trotted out for everyone's amusement. She just wasn't ready to deal with it yet. She opened her mouth to give some lame excuse about the holidays, but Warren beat her there. He shot a charming smile at Dorothy. "Now, Dorothy, you know good and well how Erin feels about those kind of questions."

Dorothy flushed, shooting her a guilty look. "Can't blame me for asking. We're all curious as to how long you're going to stay. Miss Nora and her bridge club are even placing bets." She darted a glance around. "Not that you heard that from me."

"Of course." Erin pulled at the cuffs of her coat. *Bets?* So that was what her life had come to—entertainment for old biddies who had nothing better to do than talk and play cards.

Dorothy finally seemed to realize how uncomfortable she was making Erin, because she straightened. "Coffee for both?"

"Yes, ma'am." Warren's smile never dimmed. "And whatever delicious pie you made today."

"Oh, you flatterer."

"Nah, I only speak the truth. In all my traveling, I've

never had pie as good as yours, Dorothy."

Laying it on a bit thick, aren't you? Not that Erin could argue the deliciousness of the pie, but that wasn't the point. She waited for Dorothy to walk away to hiss, "Suck-up."

"You didn't want to be in the spotlight. I made sure you weren't."

There was too much knowledge in his dark eyes. Here in the bright light of The Diner, it was impossible to ignore the questions he'd voiced up at the water tower. *He knows. He might not know the specifics, but he knows everything isn't rainbows and sunshine.* The temptation to confess everything to Warren almost overwhelmed her. Instead, she cleared her throat. "You picked truth."

"I did." He didn't so much as twitch.

She almost went with some bullshit one-off easy question, but once again, her mouth got away from her. "Do you ever see yourself doing this?" She waved at The Diner. At this time of night, there were only a few booths occupied, but in so many ways it represented everything that Wellingford was— stuck in its ways and clinging to the past…but also warm and friendly and with a great heart.

"Doing what, exactly?"

"Settling down, putting a ring on some poor unsuspecting woman's finger, maybe popping out a few screaming kids."

He shook his head. "When you put it like that…"

Though part of her wanted to clarify that she didn't think it was *that* bad—after all, Marcy was more than happy with Erin's brother—she kept her mouth shut. She and Marcy weren't the same type of person. She didn't have a stable part of her life, while her best friend was rock solid in every way that mattered. No, that kind of thing wasn't for Erin. She'd hit the ground running as soon as she found her feet again.

It was just taking a little longer than she expected.

What am I going to do with my life now?

That was the million-dollar question.

Warren shrugged out of his coat and set it on the seat beside him, and then leaned back and stretched his arms over the booth. It brought her attention to the truly spectacular cut of his chest. Guilty, she forced herself to look at his face…only to find him watching her. He gave a slow grin that made her stomach erupt into butterflies. "Like what you see?"

"Sure—as long as I forget who it's attached to." The words didn't come out nearly as sharp as she intended. Instead, they were soft and almost pleading. *Get your shit together, Erin.* "You're stalling. Answer the question."

"I'm not stalling." He shrugged. "And I don't know. If I could settle down anywhere, it would be in this town. My granddad's here, and he'd be tickled pink if I got married and gave him some great-grandbabies to spoil." He paused while Dorothy brought their coffee and pie and shuffled off. "But I can't help but wonder if there's too much of my parents in me to ever make that work. If I'll wake up one day with that itch to move, and it'll eventually drive a wedge through me and any theoretical wife."

He was looking at her far too intently. She took a hasty sip of her coffee and choked when she found it just this side of scalding. Warren didn't rush to fill the silence that descended between them, though. He just kept watching her with that strange expression. She touched her mouth. "Do I have something on my face?"

"No." Just that. Nothing to give her any clue into what the hell he was thinking.

She took another sip, more carefully this time. *Well, this is awkward.* "Warren—"

"You can talk to me, Freckles. I know we aren't exactly best friends, but if there's anyone in this town who will understand without judging, it's me."

Understand? Probably. Be able to keep his mouth shut

and not make her feel even worse? That was the part up for debate.

Erin stared into her coffee, but it didn't magically provide any answers. The truth was, she didn't have a single damn person to talk to. Her parents tried their best, but everything they said was colored with the fact that they wanted her to move back here permanently more than anything else in the world. Aaron would try, too, but everything was so cut-and-dried with him. He loved being a deputy and he loved Marcy and her daughter with everything he had. It never occurred to him that not everyone dreamed of a life like that. And Marcy…Marcy was just as bad as Aaron in her own way. As glad as Erin was for both her best friend and her brother's happiness…a part of her definitely felt left on the outside.

She sipped her coffee, but it bought her a grand total of two seconds. This was it. She could shut him down and he might actually back off for good…or she could take a tiny leap of faith and see what happened. She glanced up to find Warren watching her again. *It's not forever. It can't be.*

But it could be for tonight.

Maybe if she thought that enough times, she'd actually believe that she could shut off the tumultuous feelings that showed up every time *he* did.

She sighed. "They kicked me off the show. I had a starring role and I couldn't keep my mouth shut long enough to actually see opening night."

"What did they do to push you over the edge?"

She blinked. Everyone else who knew the truth had instantly jumped in with how she never managed to keep her temper under wraps, all seeming to imply that it was totally and completely her fault that this happened. And it was. She hadn't managed the self-control to keep from laying into Randy. "What makes you think it was provoked?"

"I know you, Freckles. You've been working toward

a starring role for years—you wouldn't just shit that away without a damn good reason, temper or no."

She took a bite of her pie and had to close her eyes while she savored the cinnamon and apple, perfectly balanced by flaky homemade crust. By the time she could focus again, Warren was halfway through his slice. *What did he ask?* Oh, yeah. What Director Douche did. "So you know how in *The Little Mermaid* there's Flounder? Well, the girl playing it is maybe twelve and sweeter than anyone has any right to be. Everyone loves her, and she works her ass off. She's better than some of the adults I've seen." It made her angry just thinking about all that talent being crushed under Director Douche's shitty attitude. "The director is one of those old school 'it takes a firm hand, spare the rod and spoil the child' kind of personalities. She screwed up one single line and he laid into her harshly enough that even the most badass actors on stage were shocked. And no one said a damn thing."

"You did."

"And look at me now. Fired, homeless—" The surprised look on his face had her filling in. "Yep, homeless. Turns out being a starving actor isn't all that glamorous, and landlords don't like being paid in smiles."

"I'm sorry." He actually sounded like he meant it.

"Me, too." She sat back, her appetite gone. "I thought I had finally reached the tipping point. This was going to be the role that made me, the one that opened doors I've been banging against for years. And now it's all gone. If I go back now, I'm going to be starting over from scratch—from less than scratch. Can you be lower than rock bottom? Because I'm pretty sure that's where I am right now."

"Do you want to go back?" He didn't ask it like he had an opinion one way or another. Another change of pace.

She sat back and made herself really contemplate it. "I don't know. My instinctive reaction is to say 'hell yes,' but that's as much my contrary nature as anything else." She sighed. "I love Broadway. I love being on stage and the high that comes from performing. There's nothing in the world like it. I don't want to give that up."

"I'm sensing a 'but' coming."

Because there was one. "But I don't miss the rat-infested apartment with the creepy landlord, and I don't miss the drama that comes when you have any number of actors together." She poked at her pie with her fork. "So, yeah, I don't know."

"You'll figure it out." There was absolutely no doubt in his tone or face. He believed she would get her shit together. He might actually be the only one in her life to have that unrelenting belief in her.

Realizing that made her stomach twist up in knots.

For the sixty-fifth time in the last few days, she wondered what she would do if she weren't trying to be a Broadway actress. Drama was in her blood. She'd never be happy with a boring desk job or something monotonous.

A thought drifted up from somewhere inside her. *I wonder if Wellingford's high school has a drama department?*

It wasn't an answer. It wasn't a plan. But it was a tiny light in the sea of darkness she'd been drifting in ever since Director Douche handed over her walking papers. "You're right. I will figure it out." Saying it aloud lifted a weight off her chest that she hadn't been aware of. She took a deep breath and offered him a smile.

Chapter Eight

Warren knew he was playing with fire, but hell if that didn't make the whole thing that much more enticing. Judging from the unsure look on her face, he'd gotten through to Erin, at least a little. Now was the time to dial it back. If he pushed too hard now, she'd instinctively dig in her heels, and he'd have lost what little ground he gained tonight.

So he paid for their pies and coffee and pasted a cocky smirk onto his face. "You tapping out?"

"You wish. No, I'm not going to be the one losing tonight."

That's what he was afraid of. He pushed the thought away. "All right then. Truth or dare, Freckles?"

Her grin made him think filthy thoughts. "Dare. Naturally."

"Naturally." The word made him laugh, because he knew exactly where to take this. *All natural.* "I dare you to go skinny-dipping."

"Skinny-dipping?" She looked around and lowered her voice. "I know we don't always get along, but I didn't think you had it out for me. If I get in water tonight, I'm going to die of hypothermia before you can strip naked and warm me up."

The thought of getting them both completely naked and rubbing up against each other was a tantalizing one. He kept his expression serious. "I'm mean, but I'm not that mean." He leaned forward, waiting for her to do the same before he stage whispered, "I happen to know the Richardses put in a hot tub this summer."

"Do you, now? That's some interesting information."

It was. Especially combined with them having gone down to Atlanta to visit their newest grandchild over the holidays and left the house empty. He and Erin would have the backyard all to themselves.

And he *fully* intended on capitalizing on that.

She reached for her coat. "Then by all means, let's get this over with."

But he didn't miss the way she kept shooting looks at him. Making her come in the barn hadn't scratched his itch any more than it had scratched hers. He took her coat from her and held it for her to shrug into, letting his hands linger on her bare neck. "No need to rush."

"Oh?" She half turned, her eyebrows raised. "Is there something you'd like to add to that dare?"

"I don't have to." Conscious of where they were—and the eyes on them—he didn't pull her against him. But he wanted to. Fuck, he wanted to. "I know you, Freckles. You're going to tease me until I snap."

Her eyes dilated and her breathing picked up. "You think so?"

"I know so. And then I'm going to do exactly what we both want."

For a second, he thought she might reach out and touch him, or even kiss him. But Erin blinked once, twice, and took a shuddering breath. "You sure have an active imagination."

So that was how she wanted to play it? Fine. He didn't expect anything else. "Prove me wrong. Ball's in your court."

Erin stared at the glowing Jacuzzi on the patio beneath the Richardses' massive back deck. The entire walk over here, she'd mentally debated with herself, flipping back and forth over whether she thought Warren was a giant asshole or hotter than hell. Right now, she was leaning toward hotter than hell. There was something downright magical about the hot tub, all lit up with steam rising from the water, surrounded by snow. It was like something out of a fairy tale…or her dirtiest fantasies.

Because it was all too easy to imagine going through the slow steps of stripping, feeling his eyes on her, tempting him until he snapped and took her in the warm water, fucking her against the side of the hot tub.

She suddenly wanted that desperately.

Before she could talk herself out of it, she shrugged out of her coat and carefully draped it over the vee of the wooden deck support. Then she shifted so her profile was to Warren and slowly pulled her shirt off, taking her hat with it. It was cold—too cold to be doing a striptease in the middle of some near-stranger's backyard—but hearing his breathing pick up was reward enough that she didn't stop. Her boots went next, and she shimmied out of her pants faster than was probably sexy, but even the desire heating her with each pump of her heart wasn't enough to combat the wind that picked up.

She slipped out of her panties, but didn't drape them over the pillar with the rest of her stuff. Instead she gritted her teeth against the feel of the snow against her bare feet and waltzed over to where Warren watched her, his hands in his pockets and hunger in his eyes. She slapped her panties against his chest. "Come and get me."

He reached for her, but she was already moving, sauntering across the patio and climbing into the Jacuzzi. It wasn't exactly the stealthiest of entries, and she shot a look at the dark French doors leading into the house's walk-out basement, sure someone would come investigate, but it remained still and silent.

Erin eased into one of the curved underwater seats, rotating to watch Warren strip. He didn't take his time like she had, but the show was still more than worth it. Each piece of clothing gone revealed more of his muscular body, and her stomach clenched knowing she was going to have full access to it shortly. *He's not mine. Not really.*

But what if he was?

For the first time, she didn't immediately shut down the thought. What would her life even look like if she and Warren were together? She might not be living in New York at the moment, but he was still in the Marines. When the holidays were over, he'd be gone again, and this time she'd be left behind.

What if you went with him?

Erin snorted. Right. Because she'd make such a brilliant military girlfriend or wife or whatever. No, that life would be even more constricting than the one waiting for her here in Wellingford. Potentially seeing the world wasn't lure enough to throw herself on the mercy of a man, even one as sexy as Warren.

A splash brought her back to the present. She watched him wade toward her, not sure if she wanted to make it easy on him or put up a token protest. Warren didn't give her a chance. He looped an arm around her waist, bringing them chest to chest. The strange light of the hot tub gave him an otherworldly appearance, and the feel of him pressed against her felt so good, it almost hurt. There were a thousand good reasons to push away from him, but she ignored every single one of them.

Instead, she wrapped her legs around his waist and kissed

him with everything she had. He palmed her ass, grinding her against his cock, the warm water around their bodies only making her hotter. She pulled away far enough to say, "You caught me."

"I did." He lifted her effortlessly and sucked one of her nipples into his mouth. The cold air made her skin prickle, a direct counterpoint to his hot mouth that seemed connecting from her chest, down her stomach, to her core. Each suck made her writhe against him, but the position he held her in made her helpless to do anything but take it.

They were going to have words about this…later…after he stopped touching her in ways that made her head spin and her heart forget all the reasons this was a bad idea. She'd survived after every other of their hookups. She'd survive after this one, too.

Probably.

He moved to the other breast and shifted his grip on her so that he had one arm around her waist. She barely had a breath to process that before his free hand was between her legs, parting her and pushing two fingers into her. She cried out, rolling her hips to take him deeper. "That feels so good."

"Better keep it down, Freckles." His lips moved against her skin. "Don't want to wake the Richardses up."

She'd forgotten that they were trespassing. Erin shot a look at the house, but the windows were still dark. "Shit."

"Shhh." He slid her down his body, his fingers still inside her, to nip her ear. "If you can keep from screaming while I fuck you, I'll give you a reward."

Shock had her laughing before she caught herself, the sound wild and breathless and more than a little happy. "A reward?"

He grinned. "I'd think fucking me is reward enough, but it can't hurt to sweeten the deal."

God, she liked this man. She liked him a lot. She started

to answer, but he did something with his fingers that made her eyes damn near roll back in her head. She gasped, barely managing to stifle a moan. "Deal."

"That's my girl." He kissed her again, his tongue tangling with hers. He took his fingers back, making her cry out from the loss, but then he set her down and spun her around. "Hang on to the edge." She obeyed, earning a kiss on the back of her neck that made her toes curl. Then his comforting warmth at her back was gone. "Don't move."

She watched him pull himself out of the hot tub and stride to his discarded pants. The man was a specimen of what the word "perfection" meant. Every muscle was carved into his body, ready to spring into motion at a second's notice. And that ass… Erin licked her lips. It was downright bitable.

"Like what you see?"

She nodded. "Now get back in here and fuck me."

"Impatient." He met her gaze as he rolled on a condom. "I've always liked that about you. You see what you want and you don't hesitate to go after it."

She hadn't thought he'd noticed. "That might be the nicest thing anyone has ever said to me. Now bring that cock over here and put it to good use."

"Yes, ma'am." He climbed back into the Jacuzzi and around to press against her back again. "Spread your legs."

She was only too happy to obey. Feeling him notching in her entrance was just shy of heaven, but then his hand snaked around her hip to stroke her clit as he slid into her, inch by torturous inch. She closed her eyes, savoring the feeling of perfection that washed over her. Why had she thought this was a bad idea? Nothing that felt this good could be wrong. Not right now, in this moment, where nothing existed outside of him filling her completely, his hands on her body, his mouth on the back of her neck.

"Remember, Freckles, whatever you do, don't scream." It

was all the warning she got before he started to move. Sliding out of her, and then filling her again, one long motion that had her pressing her face against her upper arm to muffle her cries.

With him wrapped around her like this, it felt like every part of him was focused solely on her. Erin had forgotten how devastating it was to be the subject of that laser focus. The man might play at being chill, but his relaxed surface hid an intensity that would have been overwhelming if he didn't keep it under such tight control.

And she got the feeling that he'd let it off the leash tonight.

As if sensing her thoughts, he growled in her ear. "A year, Freckles. An entire year you kept me locked out. A year where I couldn't sink myself into your hot pussy and feel you clench around me. Three hundred and sixty-five fucking days without feeling you come and knowing I was the cause."

She gripped the side of the hot tub so hard little pinpricks of pain sparked along her fingertips. "I know." Whose shitty idea had it been to deny herself this pleasure?

Oh. Right. *Hers.*

He slammed into her, his free hand cupping her breast, calloused palms against her sensitive nipple. "Was it worth it?"

There was only one answer. "Fuck, no."

"Come back to my place."

She was so focused on what he was doing to her that it took a second to realize he wasn't just talking dirty. All the reasons she'd avoided him for the last year fell away. "Okay."

His reaction was reward enough. He grabbed her hips and slammed into her, again and again, driving her over the edge before she even knew it was before her. She clenched her teeth to keep her cry internal. Warren's strokes became more and more irregular, until he gripped her hard enough to bruise and came, her name on his lips in a groan.

He turned her around and kissed her, the touch so gentle after the thorough fucking he'd just given her that it made her head spin. He kept his thumb on her chin, using a slight pressure to get her to meet his gaze. "Come home with me."

This wasn't a request in the middle of the moment. This was something else. She held her breath, realizing, *he's giving me a chance to back out*. It was too late for that. Far too late. She nodded. "I'll go home with you."

Chapter Nine

Warren led the way up the rickety stairs to the loft above the garage, all too aware of a shivering Erin at his back. Getting back into their dry clothes had been a whole lot less sexy than getting out of them, and the entire walk from Main Street to here he'd expected her to change her mind. She hadn't.

She hadn't been here since that summer they spent together, and hell if it didn't feel more important than it probably should. He opened the door and let her precede him into the room. He followed, flipping on the single light that covered the entire room.

It hadn't changed much in the six years since her last time here. There was still his shit scattered on the old desk and over the corkboard on the wall above it, his bed—made to regulation standard—against the far wall. The only difference was that he'd bought a bigger television and had the newest Xbox console hooked up to it.

Erin turned to face him, her cheeks rosy from the cold they'd just left. "I'm ready for my reward."

Hell, he was ready to give it to her. Warren shrugged out of his coat but shook his head when she went to do the same. "Let me."

"Warren—"

"Tonight is on my terms, Freckles." He waited while she mulled that over. It was a good sign that she gave a jerky nod in response, or at least that was what he told himself. He pulled his shirt over his head and yanked off his boots, and then he padded over to circle her. "You're beautiful. You know that, don't you?"

"I've been told." A small smile tilted up the corners of her lips.

"You should be told more often." He unzipped her coat and slid it slowly off her, then walked over to drape it over the chair at the desk.

"Warren." Her voice was closer than it should have been, and when he turned around, she was practically in his arms. "I don't want to wait anymore."

"Your reward—"

"I don't care about any stupid reward. I just want you."

All his careful planning and scheming went right out the window at the stark desire in her eyes. And then she was in his arms, her arms around his neck and her mouth on his. She kissed him with a fervor bordering on desperation, but for the life of him he couldn't tell if it was desperation to avoid thinking about her current situation or desperation for him.

He backed toward the bed, both of them shedding clothes with every step. And then there was just her and him and nothing between them. His back hit the mattress, a naked Erin straddling him. "You've been in charge all night. It's my turn."

The last few hours had been working them to this point, but this wasn't how he'd planned on things playing out. But now, with her looking at him like that, he couldn't think of a damn reason to go back to his plan. "I'll consider it."

She smirked. "You do that. In the meantime…" She kissed his collarbone, and then slithered lower. "I'll just be down here…" A kiss to his sternum. "Occupying myself."

He laced his fingers through her cold, damp hair, fighting back a sliver of guilt that she'd been walking all the way back here with wet hair after that hot tub dare. She didn't give him a chance to dwell on it, biting his stomach and surprising a laugh out of him. "I think I can live with that."

"What happened here?" Her entire tone was different. Gone was the playful edge to her words, replaced by something else altogether.

Warren didn't have to look down to know what she was talking about. "It was just a flesh wound."

"Are you sure, because this looks like a fucking bullet went through you." She burrowed a hand between his back and the mattress. "And this feels like a goddamn exit wound."

Her anger brought his knee-jerk response up short. He searched her face, shock washing over him when he realized she wasn't actually angry. No, she was fucking terrified. He ran his hands up her arms, finding her whole body shaking. "Freckles, it's okay. *I'm* okay. It wasn't even serious enough to warrant physical therapy."

"Why didn't I hear about this? There are no secrets in this goddamn town. I *should* have heard about this."

He sat up, bringing them face-to-face. "My granddad was a Marine, too, did you know that?"

"No." She blinked. "What does that have to do with anything?"

"It means that he knows that sometimes you don't talk about this shit. This was cake compared to what some guys go through, but it's still not a story I'm going to be whipping out the first opening I see in any conversation." He could tell that wasn't enough, so he kept going, baring himself to her in a way he'd never really intended. "It scared the shit out of me, Erin. I was in the hospital for a while, and it was long enough to wonder if I'd make it. That kind of thing puts a lot of stuff into perspective."

Like that he was tired of fucking around with the one woman in his life he connected with in a way that defied explanation.

She still looked uncertain and scared, so he fell back on the one thing he knew that would get her to stop worrying. "Kiss me, Erin. I dare you."

Sure enough, she frowned. "It's not your turn."

"Okay, then. I pick dare."

She rolled her eyes. "This conversation isn't over."

"I know." But he hoped that he could spend the next few hours convincing her to give them a chance before they had it.

For a long moment, he thought she might insist, but then she sighed. "I dare you to kiss me."

He wasted no time hooking the back of her neck and pulling her to him. He kissed her with everything he had, trying to convey all the things he couldn't quite put into words. She instantly went soft against him, her tongue stroking his and her fingers digging into his shoulders. Only then did he lie back down, taking her with him. "I'll even let you call the shots—for now."

"How magnanimous of you."

"That's me. Magnanimous."

She slid down his body and settled between his thighs. "You'd better have a condom ready, because after I drive you crazy, I'm going to ride you until your eyes roll back in your head."

He reached over to the nightstand without taking his eyes off hers and rummaged around until he came up with a condom. A quick check ensured it wasn't expired, and he tossed it onto the bed next to them. "Any other requests?"

"Yeah." Her grin was downright wicked. "Find something to hang on to."

And then her mouth was on his cock, sucking him down, down, until his head damn near exploded. "Holy fuck."

She made a sound of agreement, and then she started back up, sucking and licking. He fisted his hands in the comforter, fighting not to arch into her mouth, to hold still and let her do her worst. Erin licked around the head of his cock and then she descended again, her hands on his hips, her cool hair slithering across his skin. "Freckles—" He had to stop and start again. "Freckles, if you don't get up here, you're not going to get the chance to ride my cock for another ten to fifteen minutes."

Her laugh almost sent him over the edge. He didn't give her a chance to argue before he pulled her up his body and kissed her. She grabbed the condom and tore it open, and then proceeded to take her time rolling it onto his cock, a sly grin on her face.

"You're getting me back for earlier," he said through gritted teeth.

"Guilty." She straddled him, and then he was inside her. Warren held her hips, letting her set the pace, giving himself over to the slide of her riding his cock, her body rolling, her small breasts bouncing with each stroke, to watching her eyes closed in sheer bliss.

He wanted this, the sex, the laughter, the sheer intimacy he had with Erin. It didn't matter that they'd only had stolen time together over the last six years, or that she'd shut the conversation down every time it veered in so much as the general direction of talking about getting serious.

He wanted her. Hell, he'd be head over heels in love with her if given half a chance.

He wanted that chance.

Warren reached between them to stroke her clit, instantly

rewarded by her moaning and picking up her pace. "Look at me, Freckles. I want you to know it's my cock inside you, my hand on your clit, me making you come."

"As if I'm in danger of forgetting." But she said it with a smile and opened her eyes. "God, Warren, you feel so good. The best."

The best.

And then she cried out, throwing her head back and writhing around him. His name on her lips as she came was the sweetest thing he'd ever heard. He sure as fuck would never get tired of that. Ever. Warren gave himself over to the pressure building in his balls, demanding he pound into her until the point of no return. He came so hard, it temporarily stole his breath.

She collapsed onto his chest, breathing just as hard as he was. "God, how do you manage that?"

"We fit. It's as easy as that."

She shoved her hair out of her face and lifted her head to stare at him. "That's not a thing."

"Yeah, it is." It was now or never. He didn't think he'd have another chance like this again, especially not after she'd bared so much of herself at The Diner earlier. "I like you, Erin."

"I like you, too." She propped herself up on one elbow, still watching him like she thought he might start speaking in tongues—or maybe he already had.

"I don't want this to be like before." He motioned between them. "I think we could be a good thing if we gave it half a chance. I want to give us that chance."

"Us…" She gave a tentative smile. "So, what, you like want to date me?"

"That's exactly what I want." He framed her face with one hand. "Be my girlfriend."

Her hesitation only lasted a heartbeat. "Okay."

For a second, he thought he might have heard wrong. "Okay?"

"Yes." She laughed. "Yes, Warren Davis, I'll be your girlfriend." She kissed him. "Now, rest up. I'm nowhere near done with you tonight."

Chapter Ten

Erin woke up to the sight of snow falling. She sat up and looked around Warren's room, curious since she'd been occupied last night and hadn't paid much attention. She'd expected it to be like a normal guest room since he spent about as much time in Wellingford as she did, but that wasn't the case at all. She glanced at him, but his chest rose and fell at a steady pace and he didn't seem to be waking up anytime soon.

So she grabbed the throw blanket off the floor where it'd fallen while they were having wild monkey sex and wrapped it around herself while she got up to explore. The desk directly across from the bed was covered with a variety of books that made her smile—everything from the most recent best-selling thriller to a nonfiction biography on the last Nobel Prize winner. It made sense in a way—Warren was nothing if not multilayered. It was something she'd gone out of her way to ignore since she met him, because it was just another tempting trait that made walking away more difficult.

Which meant it was probably a bad idea to snoop further,

but she couldn't help herself. She moved to the corkboard on the wall next to the desk, finding it peppered with pictures. Most of them were of a middle-aged couple that must be Warren's parents in a variety of exotic locations across the world. He was with them in some pictures—a younger, wilder version of himself. *He's seen so much. All I ever wanted was New York, and I never bothered to look further.*

Her dreams had never felt stunted before, but faced with evidence of the sheer amount of traveling he'd done, she couldn't help a small sliver of dissatisfaction. Annoyed with herself, she focused on the pictures that weren't of his parents. There were a scattering of other people who must be his friends, and a few of him and another man in uniform with a desert in the background. *He's seen combat. He was* shot. *How could I have forgotten that? God, I'm starting to feel seriously immature right now.* He was never going to give this up, and she'd be a monster to ask that of him.

And she'd never be happy playing the role of little wife while he went off and had adventures.

"I can't do this."

"You're up early." Warm arms slipped around her waist, and she jumped, feeling guilty and then annoyed for feeling guilty. Warren's breath tickled her ear. "Come back to bed. I'm not done with you yet."

"But you will be." She tried to stop the words from coming, but they were like a force of nature beyond her control. Erin stepped away from him, turning as she did. He looked…God, he looked good enough to eat. His dark eyes were still hooded with sleep, and his body was even better in the light of day. It wasn't fair. She'd never held to the belief that anything could be damn near perfect, but Warren fit the bill. Last night had only cemented that truth.

But if something seemed too good to be true, it probably was—and that was certainly the case this time. Yes, last night had been amazing, and yes, she wanted a whole life of nights like that with this man. She wanted it so desperately it made her shake.

It wasn't in the cards, though.

He was shot. *He might want to be with me more than anything else in the world, but it won't make a damn bit of difference to the next bullet headed in his direction. He could die the next time they send him over there. And they will. It's only a matter of time.*

Warren frowned, zeroing in on her as the last of the relaxation leached out of him. "Whatever you're thinking, stop it."

"It's not that simple. You can't just wave a magic wand at a situation and make it all perfect."

"Erin—" He stopped and seemed to make an effort to control his tone. "Talk to me. We'll figure it out."

"There's no figuring this out. I know I'd said I'd be your girlfriend, but…" They were on two different paths. They always had been. Last night might have tricked her into believing that they could have some sort of future together, but the only way that was possible was to sacrifice everything she cared about on the altar of love. *I can barely stand the thought of the world without him, and he's only been on the periphery of my life. Having him—really having him—with me and then losing him would destroy me.* "I have to go."

"No, you don't." He moved between her and the door. "You're not going to walk out of here before you talk to me and tell me what the hell is going through that crazy brain of yours. Last night you were all about finding a way to make this work. Tell me what changed."

"If a guy can't be held accountable for saying the L-word while he's inside a woman, then I don't have to be accountable for what I said right after you were inside me." She shoved her free hand through her hair. "I need my clothes."

"*Erin.*"

He wasn't going to sit back and let her walk away this time. That much was crystal clear. She dropped the sheet and went for her pants. *Say something. Say whatever it takes to get him to let you walk out of here.* She grabbed at the first thing she could think of. "What would our future even look like?"

"I don't know. We'll figure it out."

It was tempting to just let him comfort her, but that was giving in to the lie. "I'll tell you what it'll look like. You're going back to…where are you even stationed right now?"

"Virginia." He sounded like he was speaking through a clenched jaw, but she didn't risk so much as a glance.

"Right. Virginia. You're going back there at the end of your leave, and I'm staying here until I figure out what my next step is. But let's say it's a best-case scenario and we try to do this long distance. How the hell is that going to work? I don't have money. I don't have a job. God, I don't even have my own place right now. So you're going to, what, pay for me to come out and bang your brains out every once in a while to keep the itch at bay? Or maybe you'll try to come back into town once every few months and we'll shack up here, in your room that your grandpa keeps for you." She motioned to encompass the place. "No, Warren. It won't work."

"Well, hell, Freckles—it's not going to work with you shooting it in the foot before we're even out of the gate." He ran a hand over his face. "We'll figure it out."

We'll figure it out. The death knell of any long-distance relationship. Because there would be no figuring it out. They'd start off strong, and things wouldn't be too bad. But so slowly that neither one of them noticed it, the little stuff would start to slide. They wouldn't text or call as much. Life would get in the way. And, before either of them knew it, the whole thing would be over. She tried to swallow past her painfully dry throat. "I'm sorry." *If I don't have you, I can't lose you.*

"Not that sorry if you're pulling this shit." He paced from one side of the room to the other. "Last night was fun."

Where's he going with this? "Fun isn't enough."

He spun to face her. "And what would be enough? For me to get out of the Marines and move to New York so you can continue to be a failed actress?"

"What?" She could barely wrap her mind around the fact that he'd gone *there*. "We had one night, Warren. Yeah, it was a great night, but it's not like we've had this long relationship and I'm ditching out." She shoved her hair back. "And seriously, if you're trying to convince a woman to give you a shot, maybe don't lump yourself in with everyone else in her life who thinks she's a failure." Maybe it wasn't fair, but last night he'd told her that he had every bit of faith that she'd figure things out and land on her feet. She hadn't realized just how much his opinion meant to her until he yanked it out from under her like a rug. *He didn't mean any of it. He was just saying whatever it took to get back into my pants. And I ate it up like a sex-starved idiot.* "I have to go."

"Erin—"

"I'd say it was nice seeing you again, but this morning would make a liar out of me." She grabbed her coat and stepped around him. This time he let her go. Erin stopped in the doorway. "Have a nice life, Warren. I really do wish you the best, even if you can't do that for me." Then she shut the door and hurried down the stairs. It was still early enough that no one was out and about as she sneaked out of Old Joe's house and speed-walked back to her parents.

Or so she thought until she closed the front door softly behind her and turned around to find her mom standing at the bottom of the stairs.

Chapter Eleven

Erin braced herself for an interrogation—they'd gone through this song and dance more times than she could count when she was in high school—but her mom just offered a small smile. "Coffee?"

"Please." It wasn't like she was going to sleep, and going up to hide in her room would just give her too much time to obsess over every second of last night and wonder where it had all gone wrong.

That's easy. It went wrong the second you agreed to that first dare.

Erin sat on the counter while her mom put on a pot of coffee, taking the opportunity to study her mother. She looked good despite the early morning. Sometime in the last year, she'd started doing Zumba and taking a bunch of classes at the local gym, and it'd put a bit of spring back into her step that Erin hadn't even noticed was missing. *I've missed a lot by being gone so much.* Great. The last thing she needed was a guilt trip on top of her shitty-ass morning—even if she was the one delivering it.

"How was your date?"

She snorted. "There wasn't one."

"Oh?" Her mom poured two cups of coffee, dumped three teetering spoonfuls of sugar into one, and passed it over. "I'd assumed it went rather well since you were trying to sneak through the front door at five in the morning."

She started to brush the whole subject off, but something stopped her. Maybe it was Warren's words still rattling around in her head, but she wanted to prove to herself that she wasn't being irrational and scared. She was being smart for once in her life. "I ran into Warren Davis."

"Old Joe's grandson?" Her mom looked positively delighted. "He's such a nice boy. I've always thought that."

"There's nothing nice about him."

"Erin Laurie, you watch your tone." She picked up her mug and gave Erin a stern look. "He's been nothing but kind and respectful every time I've encountered him, even with your brother acting a damn fool every time he sets sights on that boy. Anyone else would have gone to the sheriff by now and complained, but not Warren."

"As great as it is to hear you sing his praises, that's actually not anything I need to stand here and listen to." Why had she thought she could talk to her mom about this? They'd never had that kind of relationship. When Erin wanted to talk about boys, she always went to Marcy, even though nine times out of ten, Marcy was just as clueless as she was. "I need a shower."

"Honey, stop. I'm sorry. You were going to say something and I just went off on a tangent." Her mom had the grace to look apologetic. *That's new.* She offered a smile. "Please. Tell me what you were going to say. I promise I'll keep my unpopular opinions to myself."

Though that still wasn't the most ideal of situations, Erin recognized it for the olive branch it was. "I like him, Mom. Even if he is a dick."

Her mom made a noise terrifyingly like a thirteen-year-old girl. "Oh, that's wonderful."

"No, it's not."

Instantly, her smile disappeared. "Okay, it's not... Why is it not wonderful? He's gorgeous and has a career and is respectful...and I'm doing it again, aren't I?"

Erin sighed. She couldn't even be irritated. Because her mom was right. Warren *was* the full package in a lot of ways. He just wasn't the full package for her. "He's not for me."

"Why not?" Her mom held up her hands. "I promise, it's a legitimate question. If you like him, what's stopping you?"

She took a sip of her coffee and nearly groaned. Mom had always made the best coffee, and this morning was no exception. "He's in the Marines."

"Yes, I'm aware."

"That means he's always going to be traveling—and that's not even getting into deployments. So either I'm traveling with him, and relying solely on him for everything, or I'm sitting at home, waiting for some uniformed guys to show up on my doorstep and tell me that this time, the bullet did its job." Her breath caught and she forced a long exhale. *Keep it together.* "Long-distance relationships don't work, Mom. They just don't."

Her mom pressed her lips together. Erin knew that look. It meant she was trying valiantly to keep her mouth shut on something she knew her daughter wouldn't like to hear. She gritted her teeth. "Just spit it out."

"I don't want to make you angry."

"Since when?"

"That's not fair." She picked up her mug. "Your teenage years weren't always...smooth sailing, but I've wanted nothing but the best for you."

She knew that. Really, she did. It was just that her parents' over-the-top enthusiasm about her shows only made her current failure that much more devastating. Because they'd done their best to support her in pursuing her dreams, even if they didn't really understand said dreams. "I know, Mom."

"I just think…" Another sip of coffee. "It might be possible that you're getting ahead of yourself."

Erin blinked. "What?"

"Warren is a nice boy, and it's obvious that you care about him. But you spent one night together." She held up her hand. "And as much as I support you, I dearly do *not* want to hear details that confirm or deny what exactly you were doing with that boy. But the point stands—you spent a very small amount of time with him and you're jumping five years down the road and deciding it won't work—or worse, that something will happen to him. Life decisions shouldn't be made based on a single night's events."

That was the thing. It wasn't a single night that had formed her feelings for him. This realization was six years in the making. Ever since that kiss in the river when they were nineteen. "I really, really care about him."

"I'm not saying you don't. What I'm saying is that it wouldn't hurt you to take things one day at a time. You never know what the future will hold—none of us do." She crossed over and framed Erin's face with her hands. There were new lines around her mother's eyes, but they only seemed to accentuate her beauty. "Honey, you have a habit of deciding on a course and jumping in with everything you have. It's amazing to watch, but it's not always rational. I'd hate for you to miss a chance at happiness because you moved too fast and spooked yourself."

"Mom—" What could she say? That it didn't matter if she and Warren took things one day at a time or not, because the majority of the potential conclusions were *bad*? That she already cared about him too much? That when things between them exploded in an inevitable end, he'd take her heart with him when he left? "I just don't know."

"That's the beauty of life, honey. You don't have to make a decision right now." She let go of Erin's face and wrapped an arm around her waist. "Why don't you let it go for a few days? It's Christmas Eve and there are sugar cookies to bake and frost."

It had always been one of Erin's favorite holiday traditions. She just wasn't sure she could really let go of all the thoughts running circles around her head. Warren. Sex. Warren. Heartbreak. *Warren*.

"I think I'm going to go back to school." She hadn't even realized she was going to say the words until she blurted them out.

Her mom smiled. "If that's what you want to do, I think that's a wonderful idea. It's funny, isn't it? Life has a way of taking a bad thing and turning it into an opportunity that we never would have considered if we hadn't been forced to."

"Yeah." She swallowed hard. The idea of getting control of her life again wasn't the big sigh of relief she'd been expecting. All she could focus on was the look on Warren's face when she said it would never work.

She wasn't sure she'd escaped the heartbreak at all.

"It's time to talk about it, son."

Warren looked up from his beer to find his granddad watching him with *that* look on his face—the one that said this conversation was happening whether he liked it or not. Old Joe knew the importance of a good brood, though, which was probably why he'd waited a full twenty-four hours to yank Warren out of it. He sighed. "It's Christmas Eve. You don't need my bullshit muddying up the day."

"On the contrary—Christmas Eve is just the day to work

out messes like the one you have going on in your head. That way you're starting fresh for Christmas itself." He sank onto the couch next to Warren with a groan. "Never get old, my boy. It's hell on the bones."

He managed a laugh. "You told me yesterday that getting old was the best thing that ever happened to you because you can say whatever you damn well please and no one can get a word in edgewise."

"Well, there's that." He raised his beer bottle in a toast and then took a deep drink. Waiting.

Warren fought back another sigh. No one was better at waiting out an unwanted conversation than his granddad. This was happening, whether he wanted to dig into it or not, so he might as well just get it over with. "You know Erin Robinson?"

"How could I not? Martha is a sweet woman normally, but I don't know what got into her fool head naming both her kids the same thing. Don't know if the girl would have had such a wild streak if not for that god-awful nickname." He shook his head. "Mini Me. Just terrible."

"Yeah, well, I made a play for her last night, and fell flat on my face this morning." He still wasn't sure what the hell had gone wrong between her falling asleep in his arms and waking up freaked out and wanting to bolt. "I don't know what the next step is. She had a pretty damn compelling argument on why it would never work." And he'd gone and lost his temper and went for the low blow. That was bullshit, and he shouldn't have done it. There was no excuse.

"Since when have you let a compelling argument get in the way of what you want?"

He glanced at Old Joe. "This isn't like the Marines." His granddad had argued until he was blue in the face against Warren joining the Marines. It had surprised the hell out of him back in the day, but he kind of understood it now. As much as he loved what he did for a living, being shot put a lot of things into perspective. A few inches up or to the side and he might not have made it. Did he really want some future son of his to go into combat and risk death, no matter how much he loved the Marines?

It wasn't an easy question to answer.

"Isn't it?" His granddad took another drink. "What was her compelling argument?"

It made his blood pressure rise just to think about it. "She says long-distance relationships don't work and that's that."

Old Joe frowned. "It might be age making my memory go, but didn't we just have a conversation about you leaving the Marines? Unless something changed and I forgot?"

"You have a mind like a steel trap and you know it." He stared at the television, not really seeing whatever made-for-TV Christmas movie that was currently on. "She doesn't know."

"Explain to me the logic of *that*."

He stretched out his legs. "She didn't give me a chance to tell her." That wasn't strictly true, so sue him.

For his part, his granddad wasn't fooled. "You spent the night with the girl and you just conveniently forgot to mention that you're relocating back here? I know you young people and your dating isn't even on the same planet as it was when I was your age, but that seems backward even by today's standards."

It was. Hell, he knew it was. But there had never seemed a right time to bring it up last night, and telling her this morning… "If she isn't willing to at least give this a shot with us in different towns, she's not willing to give it a shot at all."

"Warren…"

"No, hear me out. She didn't even give me a chance to talk to her and address her fears. She just decided that it wouldn't work and walked out. That's not how you act when you really care about someone." It didn't take much to picture the stubborn set of her features as she'd yanked on her clothes and walked out of his room—out of his life. "When you care for someone, you fight for them."

Old Joe sighed. "You and that girl have been circling each other for years. You didn't really think it would be easy, did you?"

"No, of course not." That's why he'd pulled out all the stops last night.

"Because from where I'm sitting, you gave up just as easily as you're accusing her of doing. She throws a wrench in your plans and you hold up your hands in defeat?" He raised his hands up in demonstration. "I know you better than that. Either you want her or you don't—"

"I want her."

His granddad shot him a look. "I happen to know that the Robinson family is going to the Christmas Market."

Every Christmas Eve the entire main street of Wellingford shut down and vendors from bordering towns set up little stalls selling everything from ornaments to hot buttered rum to cookies. There were Christmas lights everywhere, and the whole place was transformed into a winter wonderland. It had always been one of his favorite traditions. He downed the rest of his beer. "I guess I'd better get moving then, shouldn't I?"

"Go get your girl, son."

Chapter Twelve

Erin clutched the Tupperware to her chest, feeling stupid. There had to be a better way of going about this that didn't involve debasing herself in front of the entire town... but hell if she could figure out how. The truth was, after she'd acted so crazy, maybe a little debasement was exactly what she deserved.

She searched the crowd on Main Street, looking for the familiar broad shoulders and dark hair. There were tons of people around, but none of them was Warren. She caught sight of Sheriff Flannery with his wife and baby and blushed crimson when he raised an eyebrow at her. Yeah, he definitely knew it had been her flashing his car last night. Wonderful. But he turned to offer his wife his bag of kettle corn, pointedly ignoring Erin.

Apparently he was going to save them both a lot of embarrassment and not lecture her on the laws concerning public decency.

I was more than willing to take all kinds of crazy risks last night playing that stupid game, but he asks me to attempt a future with him and I chicken out. I'm such an idiot.

She moved farther down the street, hoping her luck would hold. *What if he turns me away?* The fear was almost enough to have her spinning around and marching home. Only the knowledge that this might be her only chance kept her going. The truth she'd realized today while she was elbow-deep in sugar and eggs and flour was still riding her hard— none of the guys she'd dated over the years ever made her come close to what she felt during those stolen moments with Warren. She liked him. She maybe more than liked him. And God help her, but her mom was right. She'd signed the death certificate on the relationship before it had even started.

That wasn't the way Erin wanted to live her life.

And the more she thought about it, the more Warren's "we'll figure it out" made sense. There was no telling what could change in the next few months, let alone the next few years. Hell, her life was so in flux, she didn't know what would change in the next few *weeks*. The truth was that she wanted to see what would happen if she truly gave him a chance.

She just hoped it wasn't too late.

"Erin Robinson."

She turned to find Old Joe standing near a booth of homemade caramels. "Old Joe. It's nice to see you." She glanced around, but Warren didn't seem to be with him.

As if reading her mind, Joe said, "He's a bit farther down." He pointed in the direction she was headed.

She blushed again, and then mentally cursed herself for blushing. Everyone knew everything about one another in this town. That wasn't a surprise. What was a surprise was the keen way Joe watched her, like he knew something she didn't. She clutched the Tupperware tighter. "I screwed things up with him."

"From what I hear, there was plenty of that going around."

So Warren *had* talked to his grandfather about her. She

didn't know if that was a good sign or a bad sign. She'd always liked Old Joe in a distant sort of way—he was almost like an honorary grandfather or uncle to many of the people in town, and she'd been no exception—but she'd never really stopped to think what he might think of her.

Or of her potentially dating his beloved grandson.

She lifted her chin. "I'm going to make things right."

"I have no doubt." He smiled. "Get moving."

She did. Erin picked up her pace, glad for her sturdy boots on the increasingly snow-covered street. She passed booth after booth, but none of them held Warren. By the time she approached the last block, she was wondering if Old Joe had given her bad directions. All that was left down there was the antiques store and the coffee shop. She frowned, flashing lights drawing her attention to the latter.

Erin stopped in the street, staring at the Christmas lights spelling out "I'm sorry." Surely those weren't for her…

But then Warren stepped out the door, a bouquet of lilies in his hand, his usual confident smile nowhere in sight. He walked over to her. "So…"

She shoved the Tupperware into his hands. "I'm sorry, too. I was an insufferable ass this morning."

"Erin—" He lifted the Tupperware and frowned. "Cookies. You made me cookies?"

"Robinson family's secret recipe." She tried for a smile, but didn't quite manage it. "With the future so uncertain for me right now, I'm scared shitless. I have no idea what I'm going to do with my life or where I'm going to end up. I took that out on you, and that's not fair. The truth is I like you, Warren. I like you a whole hell of a lot. It scares me almost as bad as the future does."

He broke into a wide smile. "I like you a whole hell of a lot, too." Then the smile died. "But I've been an ass, too. I kind of left out a vital piece of information during our time in the last twenty-four hours." He rushed on before she could ask what he meant. "I only have four months left in the Marines. My time to reenlist came up a while back, and I didn't do it."

Her gaze involuntarily dropped to his side where she could still picture the scar that had scared her so badly last night. "What are you going to do?"

"I hear the Wellingford police department has an opening for a deputy."

That shocked a laugh out of her. "You're going to work with my brother… Oh my God, Aaron is going to positively *love* that."

"I know." His lips quirked. "I got these for you." He passed over the flowers.

She closed her eyes and inhaled. Lilies. Her favorite. She'd mentioned it in passing a couple years ago, and the fact that he'd remembered after all this time only reinforced that she was making the right decision. "I still don't really know what I'm doing. I might go back to school, or… I just don't know."

"That's the beauty of life—it's always changing, and you don't have to have it all figured out."

Maybe. She gripped the flowers so tightly her fingers went numb. It was now or never. "I might not have the rest of life figured out, but I want a chance with you—a real chance, not one that I've made up in my head and then set afire. I want to be your girlfriend. I can't tell you what the future holds, but I know I want to spend it with you."

He used his free hand to pull her against him. She went up onto her tiptoes and kissed him. The sound of cheering had her lifting her head to find that they'd acquired an audience at some point. Old Joe stood next to her parents, and there was Aaron and Marcy and their tiny family. *I have roots here. And that's not a bad thing.* Suddenly, the future didn't look that scary at all. Not with so many people in her corner and rooting for her.

She looked at Warren. "Wellingford's prodigal son and wayward daughter are back in the fold and dating. I think the town approves."

His grin made her entire body hum. "It's a Christmas miracle."

Acknowledgments

To God—thank you for more good days than bad, and more sunshine than rainstorms.

To Vanessa Mitchell—thanks for understanding exactly where I was going with Erin and Warren's story and helping polish it to perfection!

To Kari Olson—thanks for the never ending supply of amazing and inspiring country music. I'm so glad we can geek out over our most excellent taste in music together!

To Seleste and PJ—thanks for your endless support and for always being there for last minute brainstorming sessions.

To Tim—yeah, yeah, you knew your name was going to be in here. Thanks for that cute itty bitty Tiny Dictator and for taking him off my hands so I can write the hot parts of this novella. Kisses!

To my readers—thank you for being with me every step of the way for the Out of Uniform series. Saying goodbye to Wellingford and it's citizens is bittersweet in a big way for me, but I promise there's more to come!

About the Author

New York Times and *USA Today* bestselling author, Katee Robert, learned to tell stories at her grandpa's knee. Her favorites then were the rather epic adventures of The Three Bears, but at age twelve she discovered romance novels and never looked back. Though she dabbled in writing, life got in the way, as it often does, and she spent a few years traveling, living in both Philadelphia and Germany. In between traveling and raising her two wee ones, she had the crazy idea that she'd like to write a book and try to get published.